"Why do we run from ourselves?

When it is only ourselves whom we know!

We seem to give into ideals from someone

else's dreams and lose ourselves!

But we must find ourselves,

yes, we must find ourselves!"

Denny Lloyd

Wherever you are...

You Are

Here...

Now!

ISBN:9798439176199

How to use this book

The best way to use this book is to open it at any random page and see what the page is saying to you!

Time is not linear; we resonate both in the past with our memories and in the future through our thoughts and imagination. But what ties the past and future together is what we are experiencing in the NOW, the present moment.

You are always in this moment. So when you randomly open the book on any page, what you are reading is a message that pertains to you where ever you are at that moment in time.

DEDICATIONS

I want to dedicate this book to all who question where they are or where they are going.

Also to those who are upon their spiritual journey and are seeking answers by following the often perilous road of self-examination towards finding the path to true spiritual enlightenment.

ACKNOWLEDGMENTS

Thanks to Denny Lloyd for his kind permission for the use of his lyrics from the song "Reflection" from his album _Running on the Spot_ (available on Spotify and I-Tunes youtube)

www.dennylloyd.com
www.putoutproductions.co.uk

Special thanks to Helen Rouen for her editing, encouragement and support in helping me complete this book.

Foreword

Over the past twenty years I have been working as a therapist using different techniques such as Counselling, Hypnosis, EFT (Emotional Freedom Technique), Past Life Regression and Spiritual Healing. In that time, I have helped clients with a multitude of issues, ranging from the very serious and extreme, such as Child Abuse, Domestic violence, Abandonment, Anxiety and Stress, as well as helping clients to stop smoking, dealing with phobias, and helping with weight management. I've also dealt with the absolute bizarre when dealing with Past Life Regression!!

In regression sessions it is not that unusual to come across trapped dis-embodied spirits that have attached themselves to clients, which takes a certain amount of skill and persuasion to get them to leave this earthly plain and join the higher realms of spirit.

I have also experienced amazing results through the use of Spiritual Healing and distant healing which is akin to Reiki.

*This involves evoking healing forces -
(universal energy or Chi) through the
practitioner to the client.*

*If there is one thing I have learned it is
that nothing is as it seems and nor is
anything as impossible as it may appear
and the past, present and future are all
caught up in the NOW.*

*Using Past Life Regression, I have
discovered that our past lives and actions
can be influencing our lives today. Even if
you are a tad sceptical about what you
have just read let's take a look at the
subconscious mind........*

*From the age of 0-7 years our
subconscious minds are like sponges, and
we take on board everything we
experience without judgement. It is
programmed by our parents, siblings and
the community we are brought up in. This
programmed habitual mind you can liken
to a hard drive on a computer. It takes on
board information without any fire wall or
virus control, uploading everything that is
said and that happens around it without
being able to filter the information.*

Unfortunately, not all the information we receive is always positive or as empowering as we would like it to be. Consequently, once we've uploaded the information to the subconscious mind it becomes the traits and habits that we continue all throughout our lives and controls ninety five percent of everything we do.

At the age of seven our conscious mind kicks in and uses this information to form relationships in our families and our external world and how we should react to it.

The conscious mind is related to our personality and is our creative mind, but if you find you cannot create the life you want or you keep sabotaging things you want in your life it is because up to seventy percent of the information in the subconscious mind is negative and disempowering. This is why it is important to be mindful and to be in the here and now so you are creating from your conscious mind and you are more able to create the life you want.

Quantum physics also now tells us we are all energy and existing in a field of invisible energy and it is our consciousness or thoughts that create our experiences. It also states there could be many parallel universes in which we exist where we choose to make different decisions and thus experience different outcomes to the ones we have chosen in this Universe, so maybe those lives are influencing us as well. The quantum Universe also tells us that once we are connected to something or someone we are always connected, meaning there is no space or distance between us.

*So while we may find it hard to grasp the reality of the information quantum physics gives us, take heart in the knowledge that where ever you are, you are always here, in the right place and in the right moment, to make or take a decision and that time is ... **Now!***

Wherever you are, you
are here
now!
In this moment!

Our inner thoughts and patterns have long been in the making and by telling ourselves the same old stories repeatedly we become stuck in the emotional response we have to them, which in turn then clouds our judgement and responses to things that happen to us in the present. When you take a moment to still your mind and let go of the constant chatter and bring your mind from past thoughts, worries and emotions you had around them, you become free from the thoughts that have been defining you and holding you back.

By sitting in silence and stilling the mind we can create a vision of the future without the limitations of the past.

So being in this moment now is the most powerful place you can be. It's up to you to decide whether to continue with living the past in the now, only to repeat it in the future or you can create a new future in the now in order to live a life that is more rewarding and fulfilling.

Now that the past has gone and the future is just a figment of our imagination, the only reality is now.

This moment.

So use this moment positively!

We are all a product of our experiences. How we interpret them is a measure of whom we choose to be. But those experiences should not keep us continually living in fear. Fear can be a good thing if we are facing danger and preparing us to fight or flight but it can also be a construct of those past experiences and emotions.

These can be irrational, and unpleasant which give us a perception of imminent danger, pain or harm.
If we let the past go, however painful, we will be free from any limitations it has given us. Similarly, we should not be held back with fear of what the future may hold for us, for this too will only limit our actions.
How much compassion, affection and love we give to ourselves very much influences our ability to receive and give love in our relationships and to others.
Once free of the chains of the past and fears of the future, we can then start to live for the present and use it to its full potential.

Don't worry!
Your life is happening
exactly as you planned
it!

As we go through life, not only do events seem to happen to us at random but it also seems that we meet people by mere coincidence or association.

Yet, if we think of our lives as a jigsaw, when we look back, all the pieces seem to fit together exactly. The choices we made, the friends we met, the places we lived or visited all helped to fashion the person we are now. So perhaps not being able to see the whole picture, it's hard to make sense of life's puzzle. Unfortunately, whatever we experience we are not seeing the whole picture and our vision and understanding is limited to the degree by the emotional attachment we put to those experiences.

These emotions keep us tied to the past and thus it is why we often keep making the same choices and continuing with the same patterns that hold us back! It is known that when we think of our past, we are doing so now, as different people to when an event happened and don't remember the events or our emotions accurately. It's believed we tend to make up to and rearrange over fifty percent of those feelings and emotions.

Only with love can we
heal the past,
endure present
difficulties and
look to the future
without fear.

We all get angry, fearful and upset at times. That's fine; it's all part of our wonderful complex nature. But to remain angry, fearful and upset is not how we should stay. It's hard to accept this when we are feeling let down by someone or something that has hurt us badly and our hearts are full of rage. It's at times like these we feel that it's justified to hold on to those feelings when the whole world seems against us. The downside of this is that those feelings not only hurt us emotionally, but also physically, by pumping into our bodies the stress hormones that over time make us physically and emotionally ill. You may feel rightly justified to stay angry with someone all your life, but the fact is they may never even know it. When you come to realise that the only one your anger is really hurting and causing pain to is you, then you can start to let go of it. Anger and fear hold us back and stop us growing into the wonderful person we should be.

It is our pursuit
of attachments that
cause us the most pain.

We all run around trying our best to keep up with everyone else or even to outshine or out smart them.
We may chase after the job, the car, the house, the partner, the life style or whatever it is we think might fulfill us.

The irony is, none of it does, they are all just the "things" that we attach ourselves to either physically, mentally or emotionally and when we are parted or lose an attachment it is then we grieve and feel pain.

Nothing is permanent and nothing stays the same yet we continually chase after and pursue our desires which we think will satisfy and make us happy. Yet happiness and contentment come from the peace and stillness within, not from the challenges that are outside of us.
Our greatest challenges always lie within us. Realize this and you are then released from the fears and expectations of yourself and of others.

Are you ready?
Is it time?
What are you waiting
for?

Have you noticed? I bet you have. Just how good we all are at coming up with the excuses for not doing what we know we should be getting on with. We listen to that little voice of doubt and fear that constantly nags away inside of us all. The one that makes us feel small, inept and powerless.

It's always ready to give us a good reason to put off that decision not to do it, you know, like it's not the right time. I'll wait a bit longer, I'm not quite ready, it'll be better next week, perhaps next month, maybe next year, when I feel stronger, when there is an "R" in the month, when the Universe gives me a sign. That's right, we've all done it. Instead of realising and accepting the time is now.

Don't let the fear of change, change you or your mind. There is no greater fear than fear itself and that of change. Go through the door of uncertainty to the door of opportunity. We are not here to be small and insignificant but to discover and recognize just how huge our power and potential really is.

The person I've been
looking for
 to change my life,
is the person I've been
running away from...
Myself!

Most of us at some point in our lives become unhappy with the way things are. We look outwardly for something to come along and change the situation for us: The win on the lottery, the dream lover or an amazing job offer, in fact anything that will get us out of the rut we have got ourselves into.

Well the good news is we have got everything we need, its simple, if you don't like who you are, the job you are doing, the relationship you are in, then change it.

You are the "soul" one in charge of your life. Once you accept this premise then you can take control of your life and start to move on from the things and situations that are bringing you down and holding you back.

Think the impossible.
Dream the
unimaginable.
Imagine the most
unlikely.
Believe in it.....
Then wait for it to
happen!

There are incredible events happening all around the world every minute of every day. Sadly most of which are brought into our awareness by an ever cynical, manipulative and negative media, such as;

"Floods Cause Havoc"
"Thousands Die In Famine"
"Pandemic Strikes Again"
"Earthquake devastates town"
"Yet another murder"

We see such headlines daily. If there is any good news its usually tucked away at the bottom of the page along with the apologies or the closing item on the evening news.
Don't let it get you down, instead look for the wonderful things that are happening, from the kindness of strangers to the love and help people are giving to others. The simple things like the magic in nature, planting a seed and watching it grow, the rising and setting of the sun or the beauty of a rainbow.

"I"

Such a small word
for something
so profound!

The most powerful word you can ever speak is I. Once uttered you are not only defining who you believe yourself to be, but also to friends, the world and to the Universe. The words we use to communicate with others or to ourselves determine the world which we create. If you continually say, "I will never be good enough," "I am hopeless," "I am useless," "I can't do that," "I never achieve my goals," then be sure that you won't because you are implanting not only onto your subconscious mind those beliefs but also the universal mind with the seeds to fail. Instead try saying, for example, I am amazing, I am really lucky, I can achieve anything I put my mind to. I attract all the right people and opportunities in my life. By changing what you say to yourself and others you will be amazed just how much all manner of positive circumstances and situations will start to appear out of the blue just like magic.

Watch what you say, you're far more powerful than you may perceive yourself to be.

The first step to rediscover
your journey,
may be to admit you
need help.
But it may take a leap
of faith and courage
to seek it!

Throughout our lives we build walls or barriers to help keep people at bay. Not let them get too close in case they see the real person. You know? The one that's vulnerable, angry, shy, emotional, kind, mean, compassionate, sad. Whoever it is we are fearful of allowing the world to see.

But sometimes we have to deal with the disguise, take off the mask we are wearing in order that we may grow as a person, and become at peace with who we are.
Sometimes in order to do this we may have to say the three hardest words that we can ever admit to ourselves:

I NEED HELP!

Strange it is how many of us wait until we reach the moment of our deepest despair, before we draw on our greatest strength to say them.

If we resist change then
we let it be our master
If we embrace it,
then we open up
to all life's possibilities.

We don't always realise it, but we are constantly giving out our thoughts which are vibrations on four levels: Mental, Physical, Emotional and Spiritual.

So, if we are unhappy with an aspect of our lives but are not honestly facing up to it or dealing with what needs to change, be sure the Universe will pick up on those thoughts and vibrations and change it for us but not always in the way we would like it to.

It is our thoughts, emotions and beliefs that create the world we surround ourselves in.

Therefore, it's much better that we face up to what needs changing and what we are unhappy with, so we can be more in control of our lives and events before they happen.

In order to move forward
you may have to leave
something behind.
In order to leave
something behind, you
may have to say goodbye
to the things you once
held dear!

Sometimes we have to be honest with ourselves and admit our life isn't working the way we would like it to.

The people around us, our old habits. Or the crutches we cling to, they no longer serve us as they did.

It's hard to let go because we fear the unknown.

Yet by entering the unknown we open up the way to new beginnings and a chance to change and grow in different ways, create unique and rewarding opportunities rather than be held back by the tired, familiar patterns that bind us to the past.

You say you have a
million tears to cry,
but don't let them drop
upon the floor.
Because in each one a
rainbow gleams,
and in every rainbow
lies a dream.......

When we are going through painful situations it's not always easy to see that in fact they can be blessings in disguise.

Tears can prevent us from seeing that what is difficult and painful now, actually allows us to grow into the more accomplished, fulfilled and understanding person that we are going to be in the future.

Remember, seed planted in the darkness is greeted by the light of a new world and circumstances in which it can grow and blossom.

Similarly, we too can grow and shine from our darkness and give great joy and colour to the lives of the people we meet and the hearts we touch.

Never doubt the
richness of your heart,
for it far outweighs the
riches of the world.

Our rational thoughts may be generated by the mind but our love, compassion, understanding and connection to all things stems from our hearts. The heart is the seat of our soul and as such it has a universal knowledge and emotional intelligence.

It is this emotional intelligence that guides us through our lives, through intuition and our "gut" feelings about situations we are in, places we go and people we meet.

It is our most valuable asset when having to make difficult decisions. It gives rise to our passions, affections and love, not only within all our relationships but with the relationship we have with ourselves.

To nurture our own hearts and the hearts of others and to nourish them with love is the greatest gift we can give.

Though you may feel
limited
by what you can do
physically,
there are no limits or
boundaries,
to your dreams and
imagination.

Quite often we feel powerless in the face of certain situations.
Which way should we turn?
What is the right decision?
Where to make a start?

At these times we need to remember that we ourselves can be our greatest asset.
No-one else has our experience or power to rise above the conditions we have created in our lives.
So, think only the best scenario, visualise the greatest result and picture the happiest outcome for yourself and for those who have been drawn into your life.

Just like an artist with a blank canvas, we have all the tools we need to colour our lives as we choose from this moment forward.

We are not limited by who we are but by whom we choose to be.

It is far better to shine
and glow in your light,
than to fade into
darkness and despair!

Strange, isn't it? How so many of us fail to shine our own light. No matter how good we may be at something, its always easier to let someone else take the credit or stand out in the front to take the applause and accolades.

Instead, we hold back, unsure, uncertain about our own strengths and abilities.
If this resonates with you remember you are as good or better than anyone else, no one can do it like you. Success isn't always measured in awards and medals, it is also measured in the taking part, the effort you put in, the satisfaction it gives you and the inspiration it gives to others.

To inspire others to see their own worth and potential is a wonderful gift.

So stop holding back, stop standing in the shadows and give it your best shot. After all, we owe it to ourselves if not to win then to try our very best.

You never lose someone
you have loved.
The only thing that
separates you is time and
space.
And time and space do
not exist!

Time was created by man to bring order to the world. If we leave this planet and travel to the stars, then time as we know it would have no relevance.

There is no space between us, as once we are connected, we remain connected on a vibrational level. Everything in the Universe is connected by vibration, from the minutest particle to the largest sun. Love too is a vibration and remains constant. Only we change the circumstances around it. When we pass from this life our lower vibration changes as we leave the physical plane to a much higher vibration and thus, we become unseen to those left behind.

Our loved ones are always near, guiding and giving us encouragement. This may be likened to television or radio waves which are all around us but remain unseen and unheard unless we tune into the right frequency.

So, take comfort in the knowledge that if someone is not physically with you, they are only a thought or vibration away.

You may seek time and
find time,
but you will never be its
master!

Time defines each moment, each life, every generation and each era and yet it slips away without fear or favour as it leaves us all behind in its wake.

Yet still we find ourselves with not enough of it, or we wish we had less of it or even have too much of it.

Time can also be like a thief that not only steals our hopes, dreams and ambitions but dampens our hearts too!

But be sure it is the one commodity we will all eventually run out of. So, if you find yourself wishing it away, idling it away, wasting it away, or worrying it away remember when each moment passes you by it has gone forever.

That is why each moment is like a precious gift to use and should not be discarded lightly. So, stop killing it and start to live it. Use it thoughtfully and wisely. Your time is now. When else would it be?

Want to experience change?
Then change what you experience!

The definition of insanity it is said, is doing the same thing repeatedly and expecting a different result. So how do you change what you are experiencing? You can change it firstly by changing your thoughts, your expectations and your limitations. Stop doing the same things, stop following the same routines and stop following the easiest path. Go with what your heart compels you to do rather than what your head, fears and misgivings are telling you to do. Be proactive in your thoughts and actions, instead of allowing circumstances to be your master and dictate life's terms to you. There are always options, always solutions and always opportunities.

Fear not the change but the consequences of staying the same.

The most powerful and
creative force in the
universe is thought!
What do you think?

Thought is an incredibly powerful vibration which creates on the Mental, Physical, Emotional and Spiritual levels.

Thought is faster than light, creating all man-made things we see and use. It gives us our dreams, ambitions and aspirations and allows us to communicate with each other. Although it can be fantastically productive and inventive, it can also be an unbelievably negative and destructive force, causing immense pain and suffering.

Knowing how powerful it can be, we should always be mindful of our thoughts, careful how we use our knowledge and think only the best, grandest and greatest vision for ourselves, our world and everyone and everything in it.

What you perceive as a
mountain,
once climbed, you'll
discover has a beautiful
view from the top!

We've all been there, facing an uphill struggle, or left with what seems like an impossible mountain to climb. Whilst the journey may have many difficult steps, twists and turns to take when we rise to the challenge before us, it's then we realize that our biggest obstacles are not the ones we perceive but the ones we place in front of ourselves.

The path to the top may be difficult and treacherous but once you reach the summit, it's then you can see the wider picture and get a better perspective. Its then you can appreciate the journey you took and the achievements that you accomplished which at one point may have seemed insurmountable.

It is,

As it is!

*When events overtake us, it can be hard
to find meaning and understanding. All
may seem lost in a sea of unhappiness,
despair and loss of control.
Yet by looking objectively we can see this
is the point where we are at, a place
where life has drawn us to, however
aggrieved or upset we may be.
It is, in fact a new point to start from.
A point with a different perspective, a
different angle and view.*

*Acceptance without judgement of where
you are, is to let go of any predetermined
fears for a future and to let go of a past
now behind you.
You are now in a perfect place to start
again; arise and use all the experience
and knowledge you have gained.
Above all never give up! There is always
another day and another way to change
not only where we are but the way we
are.*

Once upon a time when
absolutely nothing existed,
something strange
happened.
There was a big bang in the
Universe.
This sent stardust hurtling
into the darkness ever
outward into the cosmos.
Then out of the darkness
and chaos came light!
From the chaos, light and
star dust an amazing being
came to be.....
you!

Scientists now speculate that the Universe was created instantaneously out of nothing.

It's hard enough to imagine the big bang, let alone it just appearing out of nowhere. Then after billions of years of change and evolution a tiny planet called Earth came into existence and became a small oasis for life.

Whilst it seems very unlikely that we are alone in the cosmos, one thing is certain: We are all unique and special.

We are made up of the same components as the stars. We are star dust.
So it's time to shine your light and not just brighten your own life but that of everyone else you meet.

You are not what you
have been told or what
you believe yourself to
be.
You are much more than
you can ever imagine!

Deep within us all there is a knowledge which is untapped and not always realised. It waits for us to step out of our shadow and into our light. By knowing we are only touching the surface of who we are capable of being, it unlocks our potential to far greater resources we can ever wish for, it enables us to achieve so much more than we could possibly imagine.

So wherever you are or whatever your situation remember from whence you came.

All those ups and downs, the ins and outs, the whatever, wherever, the loves, the highs, the lows and the heart aches.

Let them all go.

Instead begin, restart, reset, and renew. Everything begins with your next thought and your next action.

Every person and every
event that we attract
into our lives is the
essence of how much we
value ourselves!

*Everything has its own vibration.
We too give out vibrations on the
Emotional, Physical, Spiritual and
Mental levels.*

*The vibrations we give out ultimately
attract similar ones to us. So if we look
at the people and the events we are
experiencing in our lives, it is a good
indicator of how we feel about
ourselves.*

*In every moment we are recreating the
person we are, the person we are going
to be, and the person we desire to be.*

*People, events and situations are
placed there by us to help us achieve
this aim.*

Just one spark
can ignite
a million flames!

Quite often what lies before us seems more daunting and difficult than what we have left behind us.
Even the longest journey, however great, starts with the first small step.
The mighty oak begins its life as a tiny acorn and every wave starts as a ripple.

Within you and every living thing is an eternal flame, a presence, a light that shines far brighter than any darkness or fear can extinguish or subdue.
Sometimes we may need to combine our light with that of others to give us the combined strength and purpose to overcome and outshine any oppression and any adversity.
It may be easy to douse a candle but it's hard to extinguish a fire!

When in the midst of lies, its time
to seek the truth.
When at your lowest ebb, its time
for you to climb.
When all seems lost, it's time
for you to win.
When all around you fails it's time
for you to lead.
When in your darkest hour, it's time
for you to shine.
When facing your greatest challenge
it's time for you to act.

There comes a time when we have to go through that door into the unknown and face our greatest fears. A time when no-one else can help and there's nowhere else to turn.

When we have to accept our own responsibility and truth and deal with what lies before us. Fear and inaction are our biggest enemies. By action we can put into motion the power of the Universe, conquer any foe, disperse opposition, and out of our despair, create hope and belief in the future.

As it ends, so it begins.
As it begins...
so it ends!

*Life is a journey we are all undertaking
and as we travel upon its precarious
road, with its ups and downs and its
inevitable twists and turns, the further
we travel, the more it is easier to
realise nothing at all can last.
Though we might try our best to hold
onto property, people, places,
memories and even life itself, in the end
everything is transient. Life is like an
ever-moving tide of emotions that ebb
and flow with time.*

*Life is just a continuous cycle within
which we travel through many times. A
sequence of experiences from when we
are born to when we leave this
existence.*

To inspire others to see
their own worth and
potential is a
wonderful gift.
To inspire oneself to use
your own potential is
to bless not only
yourself but all those
that cross your path!

Often, we encourage others to do their best, tell them how good they are and praise their talents and gifts. Or we might go to watch our heroes perform and marvel at what heights they can rise to and achieve. We do this but how often do we hide our own talents and skills?

We all have special skills, special ways and depths of talent that distinguish us from everyone else and yes, while we may never reach the heights of our heroes, we all still possess a part of us that is unique and unrivalled.
So, stop holding back, ask yourself (if you can't let go) what are you saving yourself for?
So let now be the moment you and the world have been waiting for, don't delay any longer.

Now is not forever!

All right, I hear you say. How can I live in the here and now when I'm going through so much turmoil and pain? I'm worried about the future and my past still haunts me.

It can appear daunting, but the past only has power over us if we feed it with our emotions. Let go of the emotions and events become just that, events, otherwise we project these emotions onto our future selves.

The future is an illusion, a myriad of what ifs and maybes, hopes and dreams.
Life is a perpetual cycle of impermanence and now is the focal point.
To live in the now is to grasp and appreciate what is real, a moment in time to realise who you really are, your power and your own strength.

The true way to affect
how another thinks is
to speak directly to
their heart, not their
head...
Know this, then you
can change not only a
single mind but the
minds of millions!

We've all been there, argued until we are blue in the face, trying our best to persuade or dissuade someone from their opinions or their actions without having any influence or making the slightest bit of difference.

It is only when we connect with another's heart, their feelings and emotions can we grasp where they are coming from and what they are really feeling. It is then we can begin to understand and have empathy with their fears and intentions.

If we connect our hearts, then we also connect on all other levels.

I love you, really?

We may find these words easy to say to the people we care about in our lives. We may also ask them to be careful or to look after themselves, not to take risks, watch what they eat or drink, remember to exercise or take it easy, but when was the last time you looked at yourself and said, "I love you" and shared the same sentiments to yourself as you do to your loved ones?

Then isn't it time now, to be kind and loving to yourself? After all you're just as important, as worthy of your love as anyone else. So, stop beating yourself up, be kind to yourself, nurture yourself, go on I dare you to. You might be surprised just how much you have neglected your needs. Look in the mirror just say the words.............. "I love you"

Remember,
you are neither here or
there.
You are everywhere!

I'm going to let you into a secret, a secret you have kept from yourself all these years. That secret is being human, you are an expression of universal consciousness. So don't be fooled by the limitations having a body gives you, because deep within you have all the resources of this consciousness, so let go of any limiting beliefs, habits or behaviours, for you are far greater than what you may perceive yourself to be. Far beyond that who you may identify yourself as. You are part of all that was and ever has been. A product of infinite possibilities and the only limits are the ones you place upon yourself.

The Universe has made
no-one else more
beautiful, more gifted,
or as special as you.
You are unique!

Printed in Great Britain
by Amazon

26096620R00046